This Book Belongs To

_____

Story and illustrations by Oryn Redford © 2022

IMAGINARY FRIENDS

Oryn Redford

Once upon a time, in a small cozy home,
in a small cozy town, played three
children called Amy, Maggie and Jack.

By using their imagination,
they could transform into
anything they wanted.

From a superhero to an
astronaut, and from a pirate to
a mermaid, and even a wizard.

Some children used their imagination to discover imaginary friends. Maggie and Jack both had imaginary friends.

But... Amy did not. Amy really wanted
an imaginary friend, so she asked
her mum.

"I'm sorry, Amy. I can't give you
an imaginary friend. You have
to find one," said Amy's Mum.

So Amy, Maggie and Jack all worked together to make a map that would help them find an imaginary friend.

FARM

My house

Crayons

Once the map was done,
it was time to start
the adventure!

The first stop on the map
was the corn field.

But there was no imaginary friend there,
there was only a scrappy scarecrow.

They looked in buckets and under stones
but there was no imaginary friend.

When they had almost given
up hope they stumbled across…

A magical land! Perhaps they could find an imaginary friend here?

They discovered a magical statue
in a glittering pool and the children asked her
where to find an imaginary friend.
"sorry, I can't see one from here".

So they asked a magical flying pudding
as it whizzed over head. "I'm sorry! I
can't see one from over here.
Maybe ask down there."

So they looked on the forest floor and found a small gnome amongst the toadstools. "I'm sorry I can't see any from down here. perhaps ask up there?"

So they jumped as high as they could until they found themselves face to face with a magic cloud. "I'm sorry, I can't seem to see any from up here. perhaps ask down by the water?"

So, they floated back down, landing gently at the shore
with their toes touching the water. Then a mermaid
popped up! They asked if she knew where to
find an imaginary friend. "Oh! I can't see one
down here but perhaps there is
one in the cave over there?"

Amy, Maggie and Jack feeling very
excited they rushed
over to the cave
to see if they could find
an imaginary friend.
But when they looked in the cave…

Rooo

OOOAR!

So shocked by the shout they began to run home!

They waved goodbye
to Jack.

Amy waved goodbye
to Maggie.

Amy was glad to be back
in her cozy home.

"Did you find any imaginary friends?" Amy's mum asked. "No" said Amy.

"But I did meet a magical statue lady, a magical flying pudding, a small gnome, a magical cloud and a mermaid." "They were all so wonderful and they even tried to help us find an imaginary friend!"

In that moment, Amy realized she had actually made lots
of imaginary friends on her adventure!

In that moment, Amy realized she had actually made lots
of imaginary friends on her adventure!

Now Amy, Maggie and Jack all
have imaginary friends!

A Special Thanks

To Mum and Dad,
thank you so much for
all your love and suport.
To all my wonderful
lecturers for all your
advice and guidance

Printed in Great Britain
by Amazon

10983691R00020